Dino Doggy

Written and illustrated by
Tony De Saulles

A & C Black • London

For Jake

First paperback edition 2008
First published 2007 by
A & C Black Publishers Ltd
38 Soho Square, London, W1D 3HB

www.acblack.com

Text and illustrations copyright © 2007 Tony De Saulles

The right of Tony De Saulles to be identified as the
author and illustrator of this work has been asserted by him
in accordance with the Copyrights, Designs and Patents Act 1988.

ISBN 0-7136-7752-X
ISBN 978-0-7136-7752-2

A CIP catalogue for this book is available from the British Library.

This book is produced using paper that is made from wood grown in
managed, sustainable forests. It is natural, renewable and recyclable.
The logging and manufacturing processes conform to the
environmental regulations of the country of origin.

Printed and bound in Singapore by Tien Wah Press (Pte) Ltd

Chapter One

Jake was looking forward to his birthday.

Poor Jake. Mum didn't like seeing such a sad face.

What about that
T. rex jigsaw
you wanted?

But Jake had enough dinosaur stuff. His bedroom was full of it. He had Triassic wallpaper, Triceratops pyjamas and Stegosaurus slippers. Gran had even bought him Pterodactyl underpants!

Jake's dinosaur models looked great,
but they couldn't woof, or wag their tails.
He wanted a furry friend to teach tricks
and take for walks.

The next day, Jake's birthday present was waiting for him on the breakfast table.

The box was too big for a T. rex jigsaw.

Jake was very excited. He unwrapped the present carefully, not wanting to frighten the…

The box contained a huge egg! Mum and Dad were as surprised as Jake.

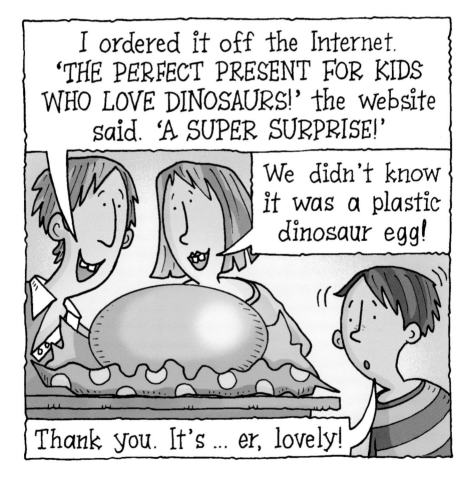

I ordered it off the Internet. 'THE PERFECT PRESENT FOR KIDS WHO LOVE DINOSAURS!' the website said. 'A SUPER SURPRISE!'

We didn't know it was a plastic dinosaur egg!

Thank you. It's ... er, lovely!

Jake tried not to look too disappointed.

Jake didn't think so. Sadly, he took the huge egg up to his bedroom.

Chapter Two

There was no space in Jake's bedroom for the huge egg.

So he put the box in the cupboard on the landing.

Then it was time to go to school.
Jake got a few birthday cards from his
friends.

And when he arrived home, there was a
parcel waiting for him from Gran.

Cheng, Jake's best friend, came over
for a birthday tea. Cheng's dog, Pongo,
came, too.

They ate sausages, dino jelly and dino
cake.

Then they went upstairs to play computer games. Jake didn't bother showing his friend the boring egg.

After Cheng and Pongo had gone home, Jake watched a bit of TV. Then he went to bed.

In the middle of the night, Jake heard a strange sound. He opened his bedroom door. Mum and Dad were awake, too.

The sound was coming from the cupboard on the landing!

Dad opened the door and looked inside. The crackling sound started again. But there were no leaking pipes. Dad moved some towels and found the box they'd given Jake for his birthday.

Jake and Mum gasped. A strange little creature was staring up at them.

Jake took a closer look. The creature had puppy ears and a puppy nose, green skin and bumps running down its back!

Jake stroked his new friend. She gave a squeak and wagged her tail.

Well I think she's half dinosaur and half dog. I'm going to call her Dino Doggy!

Then he carried her back to his bedroom.

Jake's room

Thank you! She's the best present I've ever had!

Mum and Dad were amazed. Did Jake really want to keep this strange animal?

Chapter Three

The next morning, Jake's dad looked
worried.

There's been a mistake. I didn't
order a lizard! It'll have to go back.

No! Dino Doggy
was my present
and I love her!

Let him keep her, Steve.
Lots of children have
unusual pets these days!

Jake stared at his dad with big, hopeful
eyes.

Soon Jake and Dino Doggy were the
best of friends. They went everywhere
together…

Jake brushed Dino Doggy every day.

And he tried out different foods to see which Dino Doggy liked best.

Jake enjoyed taking Dino Doggy for walks in the park. He didn't mind that people were frightened of her.

But Pongo wasn't scared of Dino Doggy. He loved his new friend.

Even Mum and Dad were starting to like Dino Doggy.

But Cheng knew more about animals
than Jake's dad.

Jake watched Dino Doggy munching her
leaves.

Chapter Four

Cheng was right. Over the next few weeks, Dino Doggy ate more and more leaves and grew bigger…

…and bigger…

…and bigger…

…and bigger!

25

At last, Dino Doggy stopped growing.
But now, when she pooed in the park,
Jake needed bigger bags than Cheng.

If Jake threw a stick, Dino Doggy didn't
always bring the same one back.

It was hard work giving Dino Doggy
a bath.

And clipping her nails was also difficult.

Jake loved Dino Doggy very much,
but having such an enormous pet was
becoming a problem.

Jake's mum and dad were not happy any more. Dino Doggy was too big for their house.

But even the garage was too small.

Dino Doggy buried bones in the garden…

…and munched all the leaves off the apple trees.

Chapter Five

The next day, Jake and Cheng took the dogs to the park.

Suddenly, Dino Doggy stopped playing and stood completely still.
She was listening to something.
Jake and Cheng listened, too.

Nobody moved.

The noise was getting louder.

Dino Doggy wagged her tail. Then she stretched her neck, closed her eyes and gave a loud growl!

Then she was off. She ran through the park and headed towards the main road.

Jake, Cheng and the park keeper chased
Dino Doggy down the street.
Her tail dented cars and smashed
windows. A traffic warden shouted out:

Dino Doggy ran into a crowded shopping
centre. She crashed through the displays,
leaving piles of clothes and broken china
behind her.

A policeman joined them as they followed Dino Doggy back outside. The chase continued down the road. At last, Dino Doggy stopped. Jake ran towards her.

Good girl, Dino Doggy! Sit! Stay!

But his giant pet wasn't listening.

The noise is coming from the zoo!

And before they could do anything, she ran through the gates.

Dino Doggy stopped at the reptile house. The giant lizards stared at her through the glass. They opened their mouths…

Dino Doggy scratched at the glass. Then there was another noise.

It was a big net.
Dino Doggy was trapped!

Jake stroked Dino Doggy's nose.

Chapter Six

But everything wasn't OK.
Nick was in charge of the reptile house.
He phoned Jake's parents and asked
them to come over straight away.

So Jake told them about the strange noise and the chase that followed. The park keeper moaned about his broken wastepaper bin and the traffic warden complained about the damaged cars. The policeman wrote down everything in his notebook.

Nick had never seen anything like Dino Doggy before. He thought she was amazing.

You can keep her if you like!

I'd love to, if it's OK with Jake.

But the policeman said it wasn't up to Jake. Dino Doggy would have to stay at the zoo until they decided what to do with her.

Come and see us in a few days.

Jake missed Dino Doggy a lot.
He asked his mum and dad if she could
come home.

A few days later, Nick phoned Jake.
He sounded very excited.

The woman at the ticket office seemed to
know who they were.

Nick met them at the reptile house.

When Dino Doggy saw her friends she gave a "Ruff!" But she didn't get up from the pile of leaves she was sitting on.

Jake looked at Dino Doggy. She was happy and safe. Although he missed her a lot, he knew that the zoo was the best place she could be.

Two weeks later, Dino Doggy's egg hatched. Jake and Cheng rushed to the zoo straight away. The boy pup looked very different from his mum.

Nick asked the boys to think of a name for the pup. Jake wanted to call him Rex but Cheng shook his head.

Jake visited the zoo every week. Herby was very friendly, but he didn't eat very much and he didn't grow very big.

A few weeks later, Nick had some good news.

Cheng and Pongo came to see how
Herby was settling in to his new home.
They brought him a present.

Jake's dad found the instructions that had
come with the big egg. He showed them
to Cheng.

Cheng nodded and read it out.

We hope you enjoy your surprise present – hatch your own Fidosaurus pet from China!

It's half dog, half lizard, and it looks like a dinosaur!

WARNING NUMBER ONE...
Only feed your pet <u>one handful of leaves a day</u>. A greedy Fidosaurus can grow to the size of an elephant!

WARNING NUMBER TWO...
If your Fidosaurus makes friends with a dog, you may end up with a Fidosaurus pup!

Now Jake understood everything.